THE CREEPER DIARIES

BOOK ELEVEN

A CREEPER CAMPS OUT

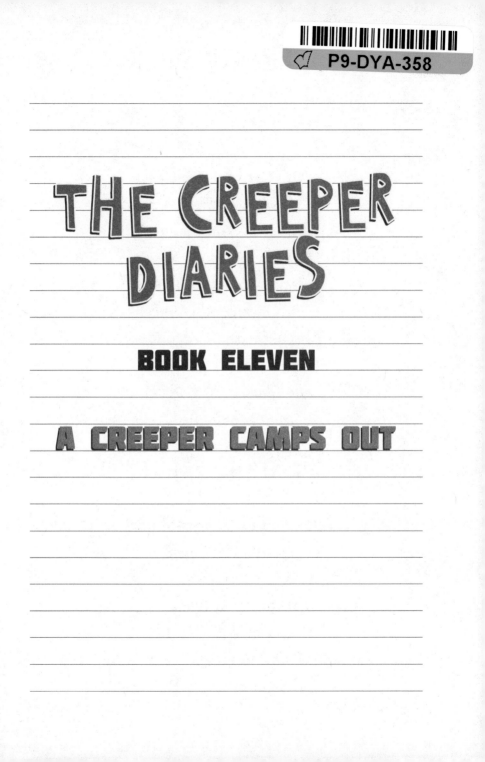

Also by Greyson Mann

The Creeper Diaries

Secrets of an Overworld Survivor

THE CREEPER DIARIES

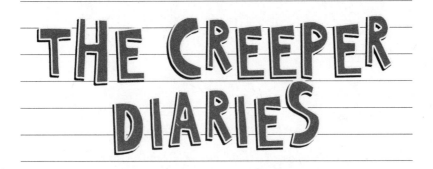

BOOK ELEVEN

A CREEPER CAMPS OUT

GREYSON MANN
ILLUSTRATED BY AMANDA BRACK

Sky Pony Press
New York

THE CREEPER DIARIES: A CREEPER CAMPS OUT.
Copyright © 2019 by Hollan Publishing, Inc.

Minecraft® is a registered trademark of Notch Development AB.
The Minecraft game is copyright © Mojang AB.

Sky Pony Press books may be purchased in bulk at special discounts for
sales promotion, corporate gifts, fund-raising, or educational purposes.
Special editions can also be created to specifications. For details, contact
the Special Sales Department, Sky Pony Press, 307 West 36th Street, 11th
Floor, New York, NY 10018 or info@skyhorsepublishing.com.

Sky Pony® is a registered trademark of Skyhorse Publishing, Inc.®,
a Delaware corporation.

Visit our website at www.skyponypress.com.

10 9 8 7 6 5 4 3 2 1

Library of Congress Cataloging-in-Publication Data is available on file.

Special thanks to Erin L. Falligant.

Cover illustration by Amanda Brack
Cover design by Brian Peterson

Hardcover ISBN: 978-1-5107-4105-8
E-book ISBN: 978-1-5107-4123-2

Printed in the United States of America

DAY 1: SUNDAY

Ah, summer. Playing my favorite videogame, Humancraft, till dusk. Posting videos of Pete, my rapping parrot, on MooTube. Helping my buddy Sam get his slime-making business off the ground (and, you know, out of Mom's carpet).

At least that's what summer is SUPPOSED to be about. And it was—for two blissful months. But that came to a screeching halt last week when Mom and

Dad announced I was going to summer camp. They were all like, "Surprise, Gerald! Good news!"

But they dropped me off at Woodland Survival Camp about fifteen minutes ago, and I'm still trying to figure out a single good thing about it.

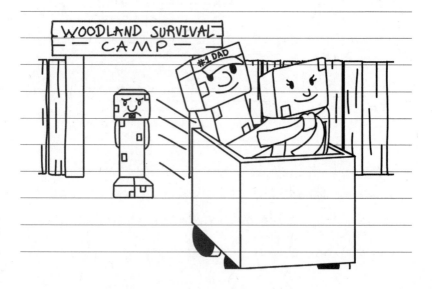

I blame Sam. He's been yammering on about summer camp since school ended. His parents must have gotten together with MY parents, and next thing you know, I'm sitting in this musty cabin, wondering how I got here.

I'm pretty sure my parents were looking for ways to get rid of us kids for the rest of summer. My older sister, Cate, was already gone, lifeguarding at some beach with coral reefs and swimming turtles.

(I know—tough life, right?)

So all my parents had to do was send my twin sister, Chloe, off to Golem Scout Camp, and throw me in the back of Mr. and Mrs. Slime's minecart with a backpack and a sleeping bag.

They're probably going to ditch my baby sister, Cammy, somewhere too and head for the hills!

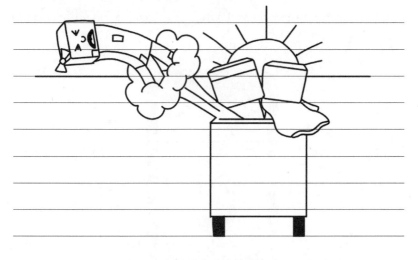

When I busted Mom about that, she said I was being dramatic. She promised to send me a letter every day for the next two weeks, just to prove that she and Dad hadn't abandoned me. I almost told her to text me instead, but then I remembered two things. First, we're supposed to "unplug" at camp. That means no phones and no tablets. (And no fun.)

Second, I do NOT want Mom texting or emailing or posting or chatting or ANYTHING with me. Not after what she did during my field trip this spring. Let's just say that I'd rather give up electricity and running water than have Mom sharing sappy posts and embarrassing photos with me (and a gazillion of my closest friends) online.

So if we're not playing Humancraft or watching MooTube videos at camp, what are we going to do? Well, let me tell you. According to the glossy brochure I'm reading, we'll be . . .

• building shelters out of twigs and stuff. (I'll put Sam on that—he was the master igloo builder when we took a trip to the Taiga.)

- gathering mushrooms. (Sign me up for that job. I love me some mushrooms!)

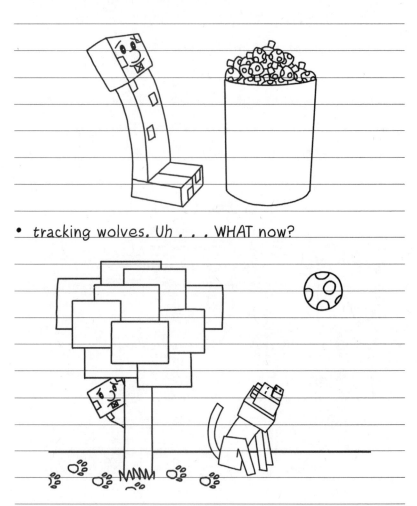

- tracking wolves. Uh . . . WHAT now?

I like a tame wolf as much as anybody (which is NOT MUCH). My friend Eddy Enderman has a wolf-dog named Pearl, and if I *throw* her a bone now and then, she pretty much leaves me alone.

But an UN-tamed wolf in the woods? Let me just say that if a wolf is trotting away from me, I'm going to let the dude run. I'm NOT going to chase him and track him down. So I'm crossing that bad idea right off the list. Okay, what's next?

- living off the land during "Survival Night."

Huh. I'm starting to wonder if my mom even READ this brochure before she packed my bags. I mean, she could have at least looked at the pictures. Kids swinging axes. HUGE mushrooms that could topple over and kill a mob instantly. Wolves with glowing eyes hiding in a dark, shadowy forest. It's like some spooky fairytale that you KNOW isn't going to end well.

"Look on the bright side," I can hear Mom saying. "When life hands you moldy mushrooms, make mushroom stew."

But there's nothing bright at Woodland Survival Camp. Did I mention that we're in the middle of the Dark Forest?

"At least you're in a cabin."

That was the voice in my head, like a mini Mom who says all the things I don't want to hear (but that are probably true).

I AM glad we're in a cabin—not in an igloo with polar bears sniffing around outside, like in the Taiga. And not in a tent full of cactus prickers, like during our family trip to the desert. And not in a cave filled with spiders.

Plus, I've got my own bed. There are two bunk beds in the cabin and then this big bed in a room all its own. Well, that bed had MY name written all over it. I mean, I had to pretty much tackle Sam so that I could get to it first. But now he's spilling out over the sides of a top bunk and seems pretty stoked about it, so . . . things ended well.

I guess I should also be glad that the two mobs sharing our cabin don't seem half bad. One is this husk from the desert. His name is Harold and he reminds me of our buddy Ziggy Zombie back home—except Harold has a serious suntan and bleached blond hair. Hopefully he's not a huge fan of rotten flesh, like Ziggy is. (I'm crossing my toes that out there in the desert, they skip the flesh and eat cactus and stuff instead.)

Anyway, the other kid in our cabin is Duke Skellington. Now I'm not normally a fan of skeletons—NOT AT ALL. There's this bully of a skeleton at school named Bones, and he's pretty

much my least favorite mob in the whole entire
Overworld.

But Duke's not like that. He came in smiling and
humming some jazzy tune.

He didn't look like the kind of skeleton who would
flick things at me with his bony fingers, or hop the
nearest spider and turn into one of those spider
jocks that think they rule the school. We'll see,
though. I mean, it's only Day 1.

UH-OH. So much for looking on the bright side. Our counselor just walked in—or TELEPORTED in. I can already tell Mr. Ender is strict, just like my history teacher, Eagle Eyes Enderwoman. He took one look at my stuff spread out all over the bed, and he told me to pack it back up and move it to the bunk beds. I guess this bed—this ROOM—belongs to him. Well, talk about getting off on the wrong foot.

Plus, Mr. Ender keeps mixing me up with the husk. He called me "Harold" instead of "Gerald" THREE times, and I was too freaked out to correct him.

Now I'm squished into the bottom bunk. Sam won't swap with me, and I can't really argue about it—not with Mr. Ender's eyes all over me.

There's barely room for me to store all my stuff here. See, Sam and I snuck a few "extras" into our backpacks, just in case camp wasn't all the brochure made it out to be. See this bag that's supposed to be packed with shampoo and soap and stuff? I swapped out all of those useless things for FIREWORKS.

I can hear Sam unpacking, too. That TINK, TINK, TINK sound is the glass potion bottles his girlfriend, Willow Witch, gave us—just in case we need them. She's super protective of Sam, which is normally really annoying. But I gotta say, sitting in the middle of the Dark Forest with an Enderman staring me down, I'm kind of glad for those potions.

OOPS. Something just fell from the top bunk, bounced on the floor, and rolled under the bed. Sam's SLIME! He packed a bunch of slime balls—the super-stretchy kind, the glow-in-the-dark kind, the uber bouncy kind. I told him to HIDE them, just in case slime is against camp rules. (I've noticed that grown-ups really aren't big fans of slime.) But Sam's TERRIBLE at hiding things. He can keep a secret for like two seconds before he bursts. So I shouldn't

have been surprised when that slime ball went
whizzing by.

Anyway, I'm waiting for Mr. Ender to teleport over
and check it out. He's looking this way—I can feel
his eyes on the back of my head. OH, CRUD. He's
standing right by my bunk!

PHEW!!! That was a close call. Just as Mr. Ender bent
over to look under the bed, the dinner bell rang.
SAVED BY THE BELL!

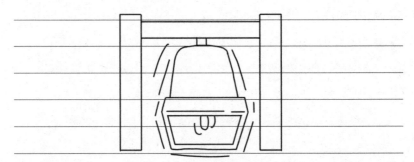

We're off to dinner now, so time to pack you up, my trusty journal. I gotta help Sam pack up those slime balls, too. If we're going to survive two weeks of survival camp, we need to get back on Mr. Ender's good side—PRONTO.

DAY 1: SUNDAY (CONTINUED)

Well, so much for getting back on Mr. Ender's good side. ARGH!

Just as we were leaving the cabin for dinner, he pulled me and Sam back inside. He found the slime ball under the bed, and THEN found the other slime balls in Sam's backpack. He didn't even have to climb up to the top bunk to do it. He just reached up with those freakishly long arms and pulled the pack down.

And, YES, he found the potions, too. And the fireworks in my backpack. And he said ALL of those things were "against camp rules."

"WHAT's against camp rules?" I thought. "Having FUN?" Except I didn't just think it. I accidentally said it out loud.

Mr. Ender narrowed his eyes and said, "Not funny, Harold." Then he dragged us off toward the dinner hall.

By the time we got there, we were WAY late and there was nothing left but crumbs. Sam ate a skinny chicken leg and a few wrinkled potatoes. But I decided to go on a hunger strike. If Mr. Ender saw me withering away like a melon on an un-watered vine, maybe he'd feel bad and give us back our stuff.

Hunger
Strike

That was my plan anyway. But he teleported to the counselors' table and left me alone with my grumbly stomach. So I finally ate a dried-out piece of fish. I mean, a creeper really has to keep up his strength at a place like this.

Hunger Strike

That's when I finally looked around the room and realized something. Sam and I had landed in a camp full of ILLAGERS.

Now I've never met an Illager in my life—probably because those mobs like hanging out in the Dark Forest, and I . . . really don't. They look a lot like

villagers, except their skin is grey and *they have*
these big, bushy eyebrows.

I'm not gonna lie—sitting close to mobs that look
like villagers kind of freaked me out. I mean,
villagers and creepers don't exactly get along.

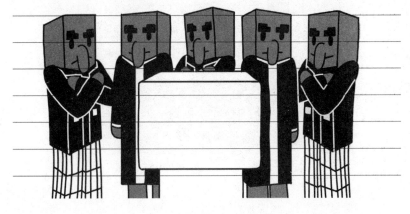

One table was full of Evokers, in their long black robes.

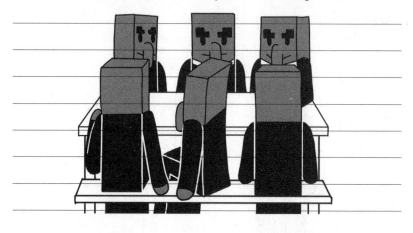

The other was full of Vindicators. They sat around like tough guys with their arms crossed. I'm pretty sure they were hiding something they DIDN'T want the counselors to see.

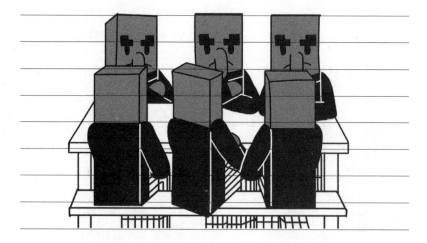

But Sam seemed totally INTO those Illagers. When he whispered to me that they looked like witches, I figured out why. It's a LOVE thing. Sam is so into Willow Witch that any mob that reminds him of her is instantly his BFF. Especially the Evokers. One of them waved his arms in the air, casting a spell, and I swear little bubbles floated over his head just like Willow when she uses one of her potions.

I was curious about what kind of spell he'd cast, but Mr. Ender teleported over and shut that spell right down. Then he gave us this HUGE long speech about camp rules.

"No spells," he said to the Evokers.

"No axes at the dinner table," he said to the Vindicators. Is THAT what they were hiding behind their crossed arms?

"No blowing up," he said to me, as if I were the kind of creeper that ran around with a half-lit fuse.

"And NO slime balls," he said to Sam, who got so jittery I thought he was going to wiggle right off his chair and go SPLAT on the floor.

When Mr. Ender called the other counselors up to the front of the room, that Enderman suddenly looked a LOT less scary. Because get this: the other two counselors were VINDICATORS. Yup, thick eyebrows. Glowing green eyes. Crossed arms (probably hiding axes). The whole bit.

So if I *thought* we were going to have ANY fun at camp, that hope just popped like a potion bubble drifting out of a cauldron.

My cabin buddies, Duke and Harold, didn't exactly look thrilled either. Duke finally stopped humming. His mouth gaped wide open, taking it all in. And Harold? Well, he looked like he might shrivel up with fright and blow away, like a speck of dust in the wind. But Sam kept gazing at that table full of Evokers as if they were Willow's long-lost cousins. Someone's really gotta look out for that poor love-struck slime.

Sitting there in that room full of Illagers, I had to wonder again—did my parents actually read the brochure for this place? I'm pretty sure this is an ILLAGER camp, and the counselors only let the rest of us in so that the Illagers would have some mobs to pick on.

Plus, it shouldn't be called a "survival camp." After Mr. Ender told us more about what we'd be doing, it sounded more like the survivor SHOW—the reality TV show Mom watches called OVERWORLD SURVIVOR.

Because we're not just going to learn how to survive out here. We'll be COMPETING against the other cabins.

Mr. Ender was all like, who can build a sturdy shelter FASTEST? Who can gather the BIGGEST mushroom and bring it back to their cabin FIRST? Who can track a WOLF all the way to water? Who can survive the night outside and be the first one to use a map to find hidden treasure?

Okay, the treasure part sounded kind of interesting. Until I pictured myself sleeping outside in a tent with Sam. With wolves sniffing around. Sam will probably take up the whole tent, and I'll be squished against the side, gasping for air, practically BEGGING that wolf to eat me and put me out of my misery.

Yup, I can see the whole thing, plain as day. So now we're back in the cabin, and I figure I have to make a plan. I'm the kind of creeper who likes to have a plan—especially when I'm at survival camp, staring death in the face. So here goes:

14-Day Plan for Surviving Survival Camp

- Avoid the Illagers (especially those Vindicators with the shiny axes).

- Keep Sam away from them too (because the poor slime doesn't know what's good for him).

- Get on Mr. Ender's good side (if he even HAS one).

- Make it through Survival Night (WITHOUT getting eaten by a wolf).

Okay, that's a good start anyway. Now I just have to figure out how to survive the bottom bunk of this bed without a slime crashing down from up above.

DAY 2: MONDAY

So Mr. Ender woke us up at the crack of dusk tonight for the shelter-building competition. Boy, was THAT a rude awakening. I was dreaming I was home in my own bed, cuddling with Sticky the Squid. And next thing I knew, two glowing purple eyes hovered over me, telling me to GET UP ALREADY.

Sheesh. Mr. Ender didn't have to tell this creeper twice. I shot out of bed like a firework rocket. Then he shoved a pickaxe, and sent me out with my cabin buddies into the Dark Forest.

The first thing I saw was a HUGE mushroom. It was twice as tall as I was, and I'm not even kidding. At first, I thought I must be dreaming. Then I remembered that they grow 'em big out here in the Dark Forest. At least we wouldn't starve anytime soon.

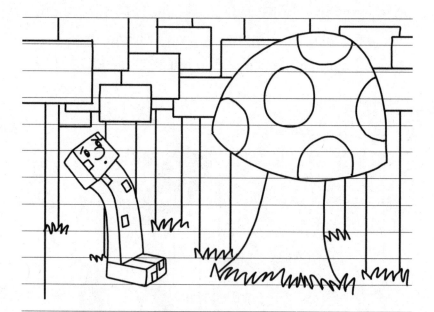

Did I mention how DARK the Dark Forest is? The trees grow so thick and close together, I thought Sam was going to get STUCK on the trail. I had to push him through a couple of tight spaces. (Luckily for that slime, I've got his back.) Duke, the skinny skeleton, had no trouble, though. He was humming and snapping his bony fingers to some song in his head.

But where was Harold? I had to keep checking behind me to make sure we hadn't lost the husk. Then I saw that Harold was SHAKING.

"What's up?" I asked him.

He didn't want to tell me at first, but then he finally said he was worried about water. I guess husks don't know how to swim. (You know, because there's not a lot of water in the desert.)

I told Harold this wasn't really a "swimming lessons" kind of camp. But he reminded me that there are streams and lakes out here in the Dark Woods, and that we COULD come upon one any second now.

I almost laughed. I mean, why worry about WATER when there are things like WOLVES in these woods?

But I figured that would be rude. So instead, I tried to take Harold's mind off things by talking about the shelter we would build.

"If my dad were here," I said, "he'd build us a MANSION." My dad, Gerald Creeper Sr., can build just about ANYTHING if you send him out to his garage for a couple of hours. He built a super-deluxe stand for me and my friends to sell slime and hot chocolate from this summer. He built Mom a chicken coop, too—and I think those chickens out back had it better than we did for a while.

For a second, I almost missed the old guy, just talking about him like that. Then I remembered how he and Mom had dumped me at this dumb old camp yesterday, and I missed him a whole lot LESS.

Anyway, it turned out that building shelters was NOTHING like building chicken coops. The Vindicator counselors showed us how to chop down oak branches and stack them together to make walls.

Except the Vindicators were using REALLY big axes, which made the pickaxe in my hand look pretty pathetic, let me tell you.

The good news is, the Dark Forest is so thick with trees, all I had to do was spin in a circle with my pickaxe, and twigs started raining down. I showed Sam, Duke, and Harold how to do it, too. Pretty soon, we had twig walls stacked as high as Sam's head. We might not have made the STURDIEST shelter, but we made the fastest one for sure.

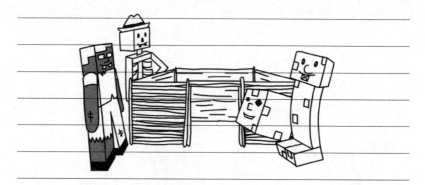

"What about a roof?" Sam asked.

That's when I had one of my genius ideas. (What can I say? They just hit me sometimes.) I found one of those ginormous red mushrooms, stood on Sam's back so I could reach the top, and cut off that round, dome-shaped part of the shroom.

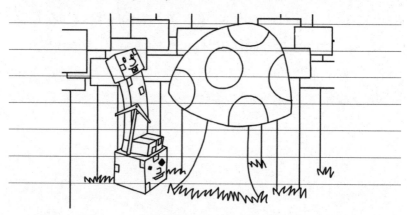

Then we plunked it on top of our shelter like a roof. PRESTO! We had a cute little cottage, if I do say so myself.

At least we DID. Until Mr. Ender teleported over and nudged it with one of his mile-long arms. The whole thing toppled over—right on top of me.

"You're going to have to build a sturdier shelter than that if you want to WIN," he said. Then he pointed toward the Vindicators, who were chopping down whole TREES. They were building a FORTRESS, for crying out loud!

By then, I'd figured out two things:

We were NOT going to win the shelter-building contest.

Our counselor was just a TAD competitive.

Oh, wait—three things.

If I ever REALLY need to take shelter in these woods, I'm just going to crawl inside one of those giant mushrooms. I'll eat my way in.

I whispered that last part to Sam, knowing he'd appreciate it. But Mr. Ender overheard me—and he really DIDN'T appreciate it. He gave me one of his piercing looks and said, "Not funny, Harold. Now get to work."

Harold Husk piped up from behind to say my name was Gerald. But for some reason, Mr. Ender didn't hear THAT. Anyway, I decided to let it slide. (When you're in trouble, it's a pretty good time to use a fake name, right?)

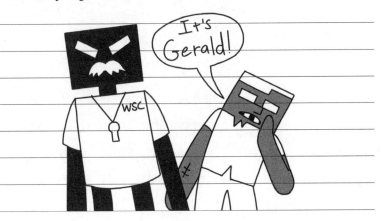

So we started over with our shelter. We tried to weave together our twigs like a thatched mat. And things were looking pretty good!

Until this Vindicator named Johnny "accidentally" swung his axe through our wall and ruined the whole thing. I guess he was hacking his way through a birch tree and the axe kept right on going.

Sam forgave him right away. (Sometimes that slime KILLS me.) But I kept wondering, what if I had been INSIDE that shelter when it happened? There'd be a brand-new ghost story for campers to share around

the campfire this summer. They'd all be talking
about The Legend of the Headless Creeper.

YEESH. I shiver just thinking about it.

The worst part was, Johnny's counselor didn't scold
him or ANYTHING! He just crossed his arms and kind of
smirked, as if Johnny was just carrying out his evil plan.

We rebuilt the shelter AGAIN. And now we're back
in our cabin, and my body is so sore from chopping,
I wish I could take a swig of one of Willow's potions

of healing. Except I can't. Because Mr. Ender STOLE our potions and hid them somewhere.

All I can do is write in my journal and RAP my misery away.

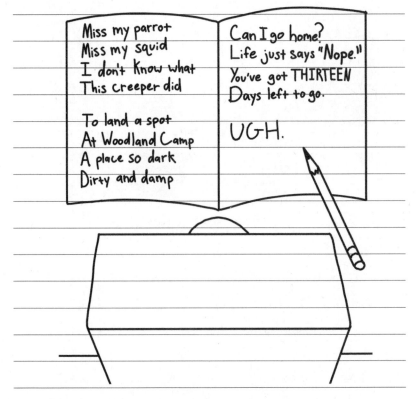

Miss my parrot
Miss my squid
I don't know what
This creeper did

To land a spot
At Woodland Camp
A place so dark
Dirty and damp

Can I go home?
Life just says "Nope."
You've got THIRTEEN
Days left to go.

UGH.

Woodland Survival Camp? Yep, you gotta love it. Two days down and counting . . .

DAY 3: TUESDAY

So GET THIS: Mr. Ender brought a bag of mail to our cabin tonight, and Mom did NOT write me a letter. Guess what I got instead?

A lousy postcard! From the BEACH!

Well, it wasn't an actual postcard. It was a *photo* Mom had taken of her and Dad sipping these fruity drinks with tiny umbrellas in *them*.

And on the back, Mom had scribbled a message:

Decided to visit Cate at the beach!

See you soon!

XXOO Mom & Dad

Well, I had so many questions about that, I nearly blew up. First of all, how long had Mom and Dad been planning that beach vacation? And why was I JUST hearing about it now?

Second, where was my baby sister, Cammy? Did they dump her at the minecart station or something?

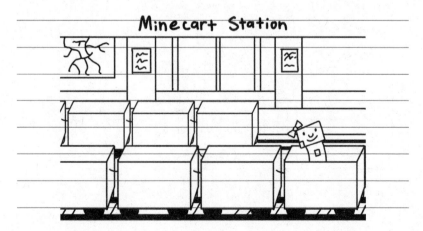

Minecart Station

Third, WHO was taking care of Sticky the Squid? And Pete the Parrot? I mean, I'd write a letter home and ASK these questions, but there'd be no one there to get it!

I pretty much had a panic attack right there on my bunk bed. I started packing my bag to catch the next minecart home, but Sam stopped me. He was blubbering from the top bunk, and when I popped my head up to see what was wrong, he showed me a letter from Willow.

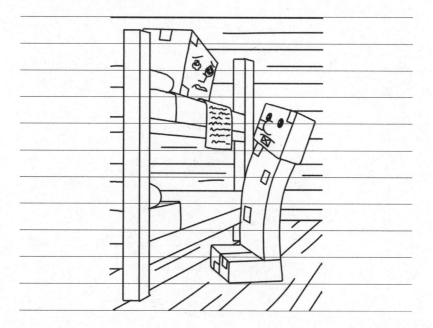

I skipped over all the mushy parts—the parts that were turning Sam into a weepy, gooey hunk of slime—and read the last line:

P. S. Tell Gerald that I'm helping to take care of Pete and Sticky. They're doing just fine.

Well, PHEW. She could have STARTED with that, for crying out loud. I was relieved for about a minute. But now I'm starting to worry all over again. I sure hope Sticky doesn't end up in one of Willow's cauldrons or something . . .

Did I mention that Sam not only got a letter from Mr. and Mrs. Slime, but he got a PACKAGE, too? Yep, it was filled with Cocoa Bean Cookies—made with love by a mother who actually CARES about him. Must be nice.

Sam offered to share those cookies, which I didn't turn down. But now he's writing a love letter back to Willow, and I'm stewing again. How could my parents DO this to me? I mean, I like the beach as much as any creep. And I'd MUCH rather be there than sitting in this musty old cabin.

"Think about something else."

GREAT. It really stinks when you're mad at your mom, and then you hear HER voice in your head telling you to get over it.

I tried thinking about something else, like about what we're doing tonight after dinner. Mushroom gathering has to be better than shelter building, right?

Except those mushrooms are HUGE. How are we even going to get ONE of them back to camp?

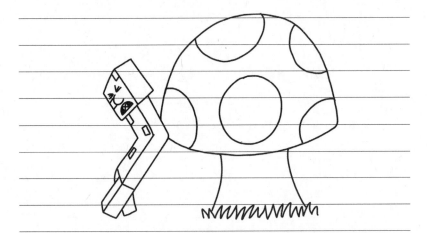

That's when I had another genius idea. (Must have been a sugar rush from those cookies.) See, I'm

thinking I could *pretty much* RIDE one of those
mushrooms like a sled—I mean, if I could get Sam,
Duke, and Harold to pull me.

If I work out all the details now, we'll be WAY ahead
of the game by tonight.

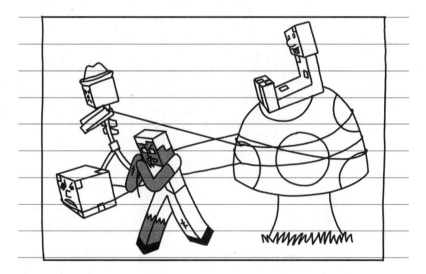

Like I said, I'm a creeper with a plan. A plan to WIN.

DAY 4: WEDNESDAY

Well, that plan backfired like a firework rocket in a well.

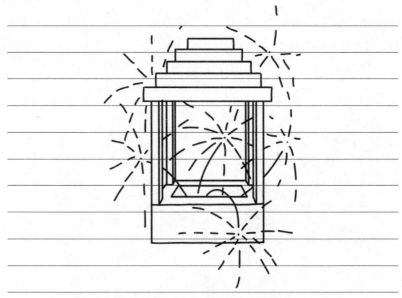

I blame it on Sam. He had slime in his ears or something, because when we were making our mushroom-gathering plan on the way into the Dark Forest, he couldn't hear what I was saying. So I spoke LOUDER.

"We'll bribe Duke and Harold with cookies," I said. "We'll get them to pull us on a mushroom like a sled, all the way back to our cabin!" Now I knew that Sam was too big and heavy to ride that "sled," but sometimes you have to sweeten the deal just to get your buddy on board with your plan.

That was right about the time a group of Evokers passed us on the trail. And when they started whispering, I could tell they'd heard the whole thing. So I figured THEY were going to try pulling a mushroom like a sled, too. (What can I say? My genius ideas spread like wildfire sometimes.)

Anyway, I forgot all about the eavesdropping Evokers while we were chopping down our mushroom.

It was a big brown one with a flat top. Did I mention that those mushrooms are ginormous? And that our pickaxes are teeny-tiny? It took FOREVER, but we finally got that shroom to fall over.

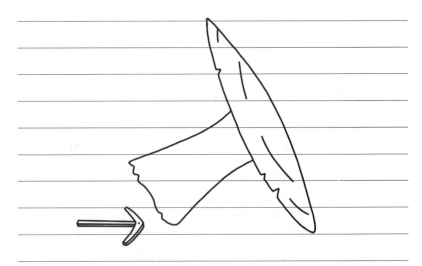

When we told Duke and Harold about the cookies, they were happy to try to pull us on that mushroom—for a payment of three cookies each. So Sam and I climbed onboard.

Well, let me just say this: Duke isn't very strong. He's really just a bag of bones. And Harold is strong enough, but he's SUPER slow. It took about ten minutes to move about three inches. TWO groups of Vindicators blew by us carrying their mushrooms over their heads like canoes. But luckily, we hadn't seen any Evokers yet—which meant we still had a chance at beating them.

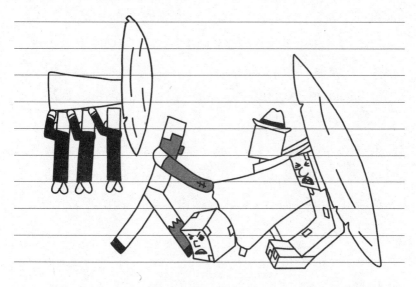

I told Sam he was going to have to get off the shroom (just like I'd known all along). But the mushroom was STILL too heavy, so I had to get off, too. We finally got the mushroom back to our cabin this morning in one piece—or almost one piece. (I mean, it was skinnier than when we started, and we lost the cap going around a curve in the trail.) But I knew there was no way we'd won mushroom gathering. Chalk up another loss for our crummy cabin.

Right away, Duke and Harold started asking for cookies, even though they hadn't really EARNED them by pulling us. But Sam was nice enough to share anyway. Or at least he would have shared. But when he went to find his cookies, they were GONE!

At first, I wondered if Mr. Ender had "confiscated" them just like he did with our slime, potions, and fireworks. But then I saw the broken window.

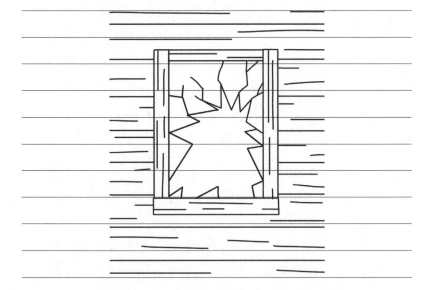

And on the ground outside the window? COOKIE CRUMBS. And a torn piece of black robe.

Our next competition is wolf tracking. But FORGET that. We have Cocoa Bean Cookies to track down first, and I think I know JUST where to find them.

DAY 5: THURSDAY

Remember when I said I was curious about what kind of spells Evokers cast? Well, let's just say, I'm OVER it.

Yesterday, just before dusk, Sam, Harold, and I snuck out of our cabin for Operation Find Those Cookies. We crept over to the Evokers' cabin while the sun was still up, hoping they'd be sleeping and we could steal the cookies back easy-schmeasy—with no mob getting hurt. That was our plan anyway. But I'm about 0 for 3 on my plans lately, so maybe I should have known better.

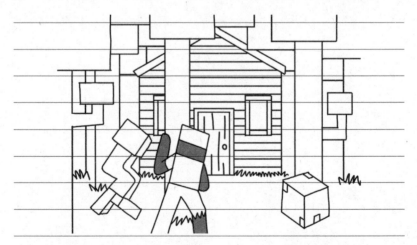

We had to leave Duke at our cabin, on account of the fact that he burns up in sunlight. We told him to cover for us if Mr. Ender woke up—you know, to say that we'd all run to the bathrooms or something (because of those suspicious potatoes they'd served at the dining hall yesterday morning). Duke seemed kind of rattly about being stuck with Mr. Ender, but SOMEONE had to take one for the team.

Anyway, we got to the Evokers' cabin and peeked in the window. Sure enough, every Evoker in there looked like he was snoozing. Except for ONE.

And one was all it took. That dude sat up, waved his arms over his head, and muttered something. Little purple bubbles floated around his fingertips—it was so cool, I couldn't look away.

Until some ferocious thing with FANGS started snapping at my feet.

It was like the cabin had grown teeth or something! A whole row of them sprang up between us and the cabin wall. Those fangs snapped and snarled, shrinking back into the ground and then lunging back up. YIKES.

Well, I've never run so fast in my whole creeper life. I'm no speed demon, but I'm faster than Harold the Husk—that's for sure. I heard him groan, and I looked back just as he got nipped in the foot by a ginormous fang.

I _probably should have gone back to help him, but it was every mob for himself out there._

I'd nearly made it back to the cabin safely when I suddenly ran SMACK into Mr. Ender. (It's hard to avoid a guy who can teleport.) And when he asked what in the Overworld was going on, I spilled it — every single detail. I told him about the cookies, and the plan to ride a shroom like a sled, and about the Evokers with REALLY big ears who heard about the cookies and then BROKE INTO our cabin to steal them.

I had to really talk up that part of the story—you know, so Mr. E would know that those Illagers were the bad guys and not us.

Anyway, he got the gist. And when I told him about the cabin growing FANGS, well . . . his eyes got that scary purple glow. Then he muttered something about a counselors' meeting and teleported away, faster than I could say "See ya."

I made a beeline for our cabin and slammed the door shut—right in Sam's face. OOPS. Harold was right behind him, so I guess Sam must have taken pity on the poor husk and gone back to save him from the butt-biting fangs. Anyway, by the time we all got back into our cabin, Duke was rattling so hard, he was bouncing off the walls. I guess Mr. Ender was NOT happy when he woke up and found us all gone.

When he teleported back from that counselors' meeting, he was even LESS happy. So I guess the meeting didn't go so well. He muttered something like "If the Illagers are going to play dirty, WE will, too." Then he closed himself up in his bedroom and we heard lots of banging around, like he was moving blocks or something.

A Rap Lullaby

Rock-a-bye, creeper,
In the tree tops,
When the dude's mad, YO,
Mr. Ender moves blocks.

When the fangs SNAP,
Your bunk bed will fall,
And down you'll go, creeper,
Sam Slime and all.

I gotta say, *the dude is pretty scary when he talks like that.* I mean, when grown-ups start fighting like little kids, who KNOWS what could happen?

We're supposed to go wolf-tracking tonight after a good day's sleep. Normally, just thinking about those wolves would freak me right out. But I've already got enough worries piled onto my brain. I mean, how's a creep supposed to sleep when he keeps picturing ginormous fangs snapping at his feet?

Meanwhile, Mom and Dad are sunning it on a beach somewhere. I gotta say, sometimes Life is REALLY unfair.

DAY 6: FRIDAY

Well, we didn't track down a wolf last night. But I kind of wish we had. A wild wolf sounds downright CUDDLY compared to what we DID run into.

Things got off to a rocky start when Mr. Ender told us WHY we were tracking wolves. It wasn't to actually find a wolf—which I gotta say was a big relief. Instead, I guess we were tracking wolf prints because they might lead us to WATER. And on Survival Night, when we had to live off the land, it might be helpful to know where to find the wet stuff.

Well, as soon as Mr. Ender said the W word, Harold Husk started shaking like a dandelion in a stiff breeze. That's when I remembered how terrified he was of water.

So while we were tiptoeing through the woods,
Harold and I were competing to see who could be
LAST in line. I finally let him win because, you know,
if a wolf came up behind us, he could eat Harold
first as a dried-out little appetizer.

I could see Sam bouncing along all happy-like up
front. Did I mention that the slime just LOVES
animals? You should see how smoochy he gets with his
pet cat, Moo, at home. He'd probably be THRILLED if
we found a wolf! Duke was in his own little Overworld,

too, humming some tune. Some mobs just wouldn't
know danger if it slapped them across the face.

When Mr. Ender held up his long arm to stop us,
Harold and I both started freaking out. Then Mr.
Ender said something like, "Harold, get up here! Come
see if you can identify these tracks!" I was pretty
sure he was talking to me. But I shoved Harold Husk up
there instead. I mean, that IS the dude's name, right?
I'd hate to steal his one chance at fame and glory.

Well, Harold pretty much fell to pieces. He clung to
the branch of an oak tree and started whimpering.
Mr. Ender didn't even know what to do with him, so

he had Sam take a look at the tracks instead. "Yup, that's a wolf!" said Sam, as if he'd just peeked inside a birthday gift and found EXACTLY what he wanted.

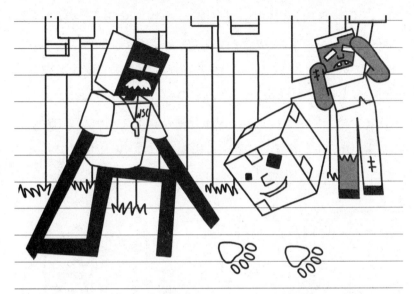

Then we were off, zigzagging through the woods, following those tracks. When I finally took a turn looking at them, I could see how FRESH they were—wet and muddy. And VERY large. How big does a wolf have to be to leave a print like that?!

I tried to drag my feet to slow the whole operation down. I couldn't depend on Harold to do it anymore—we'd lost that husk a while back. He was probably still hanging from that oak tree, frozen like an ice spike in the Taiga.

Mr. Ender was moving so fast down the trail, he was practically teleporting. And my gut screamed at me with every step that danger was right around the corner. I could FEEL it! Or maybe that was just the mushroom stew from dinner bubbling up inside. Any second now, I was probably going to hurl. But even THAT wouldn't slow down this tracking party.

Then. It. Happened.

We came around this bend in the trail, and the mushrooms were growing so big and thick, I had to push Sam between them. He popped out on the other side, and I raced to catch up with him. And that's when I heard the rustle in the bushes.

And whirled around.

And saw something LEAPING at me from the top of a giant mushroom.

When I hit the ground under the weight of that giant beast, I'm not gonna lie—I blew up. Just a little. And that explosion blew the wolf right off me.

Except it WASN'T a wolf. It was a Vindicator. That kid Johnny!

I don't know who looked more freaked out—me or Johnny. But his team of Vindicators came running from out of nowhere. And when I saw his counselor sprinting toward me with a giant axe, I nearly blew up AGAIN.

Johnny didn't even apologize. He just got up, brushed off his jacket, and started whispering and laughing with his axe-wielding friends. And guess who got in trouble?

Yup. ME. I, Gerald Creeper Jr., got chewed out by a Vindicator counselor who said that blowing up was "against the rules." Well, what about hiding on top of a giant mushroom, waiting for a helpless creeper to creep by? What about ATTACKING that creep and tackling him to the ground? Where in the rules does it say THAT's okay?

I gotta say, Mr. Ender really went to bat for me. He got all up in the Vindicator counselor's face.

Sure, he called me "Harold" a few times, but I appreciated the effort.

I guess it didn't work, though, because the Vindicators just went on their merry way like nothing had happened. But our search party turned around. Why? Because Mr. Ender had lost his mojo. So we followed those wolf tracks all the way BACK to our cabin.

I heard this morning that the Evokers were the first ones to track the wolf prints to water. Rumors are swirling that they even spotted a wolf along the way. But who knows? Maybe they just cast a spell and conjured up a few fangs to make it look good.

Anyway, Mr. Ender has gone weird on us. It's dawn—time to hit the sheets—but strange sounds are coming out of Mr. Ender's bedroom. Sam and I pressed our ears to the knotholes in the door, and we heard the tinkling of glass. Well, I'd know that sound anywhere—those are POTION bottles that Mr. Ender is messing with. OUR potion bottles! So he must be planning on using them to strike back at the Illagers.

I really think he should give me back my fireworks while he's at it. But when he opened the door and

Sam and I got busted for snooping, I didn't have the guts to ask.

Now I can't decide if I'm EXCITED about what's going to happen next, or if I'm downright terrified. Either way, things are about to get interesting around here . . .

DAY 7: SATURDAY

So I guess Friday nights are all about "down time"
here at Woodland Survival Camp. No shelter building.
No mushroom gathering. No wolf tracking. Which
meant I had plenty of time to stew over the letters
that I did NOT get from my mom today.

Instead, I got a stack of postcards. Like Mom thought
she could send me four at a time to make up for the
four days that she didn't think about me AT ALL.

I spread those postcards out on my bed—and fought
the urge to rip them to shreds. There was a photo

of Dad with a snorkel mask on, snoozing on a beach towel. Then Dad with a fishing pole, snoozing on the pier. Then Dad buried in the sand, snoozing . . . well, you get the idea. Apparently vacation is REALLY exhausting for the old guy.

The fourth postcard showed Cammy riding a turtle. So I guess my parents didn't ditch her after all—at least not yet. But I'm sure the little creep's days are numbered.

Anyway, while I was trying not to blow the postcards to smithereens, Sam was on the top bunk opening up a box marked "Perishable." That could only mean one thing: more COOKIES.

I climbed up to take a look, because the one thing that can make an unloved, unwanted creeper kid feel better about himself is a Cocoa Bean Cookie. But do you know what Sam unwrapped instead?

A CAKE. With white swirly frosting. And pink sprinkles. And a few black and white cat hairs stuck in the frosting.

Well, seeing those cat hairs made me want to hurl. But Sam? He started to cry. I guess he really misses his cat, Moo.

I told my green buddy *that* we should *probably* eat that cake right away—that it would make him feel better. He wiped his nose and nodded, and next thing you know, we'd polished off *that* WHOLE cake before any mob could steal it away from us. (I might have accidentally eaten a cat hair or two, but I don't even care.)

We weren't exactly starving when dinner rolled around, but I was *pretty* excited about the campfire. I mean, before I knew what would HAPPEN at that campfire.

See, the Vindicator counselors decided we should tell a few ghost stories. I really only know one—the story about Herobrine, the phantom miner, who haunts the Overworld. EVERY mob knows that story, so when I told it, everyone kept interrupting me to point out the details I was getting wrong. SHEESH. That'll teach me to open my mouth at a camp full of Illagers.

Anyway, Harold had a *pretty good* story to share. It was about these mobs called the Drowned. They're these undead mobs that spawn when zombies drown in water. They start to shake, and their eyes turn blue and get all glowy. They live deep down at the bottom of lakes or oceans, but at night, they swim to the surface. And if you're ANYWHERE near the water, those Drowned will ATTACK you!

Well, we all jumped when Harold got to the end of his story. I mean, no wonder the poor husk is terrified of water!

When Johnny started telling a ghost story, I decided not to listen. I didn't want that jerk to think I cared about ANYTHING he had to say. But when I saw all the other Illagers pulling their logs closer to Johnny, I might have heard a FEW words.

He was talking about these mobs called Illusioners. I guess they cast spells that can BLIND you! And when you try to fight back, they turn invisible—and a bunch of FAKE Illusioners show up so you don't know if you're fighting the real ones or the fake ones. Johnny said they've been spotted here in the Dark Forest. Was he telling the truth?

Probably not, but I'm not gonna lie. The hairs stood up on my creeper legs when I heard about those Illusioners. And after Johnny's story, no one talked for a REALLY long time.

So when the Evokers cast a spell, we didn't see it coming. My buddies and I weren't prepared. I mean, how COULD we be???

The GHOSTS came from out of NOWHERE. I heard this
horn, and then those pale, winged mobs started
swirling around the fire. When one SWOOPED at me,
I fell right off my log. Did I shriek like a ghast? You
bet I did.

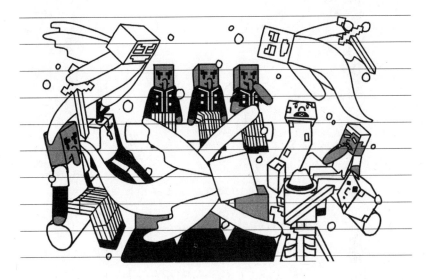

Sam was so freaked out, he melted. Duke dropped
a few bones. And Harold staggered so close to the
fire, he lit up and had to drop and roll!

But the rest of the Illagers? They just LAUGHED and
laughed and laughed. Because they all knew that

those weren't ghosts dive-bombing us. They were VEXES, a spell the Evokers had cast.

When the spooky vexes finally disappeared, my buddies and I were ready to take our drops and go home. But that's when two purple eyes appeared in the darkness—staring RIGHT AT ME.

Mr. Ender.

He teleported over and sat on my log. He turned to face me with those creepy glowing eyes. And then he said two words.

He led us back to our cabin, and then he dumped out our bag of potions and pointed at me. "Harold," he said, "it's time for you to tell us about these potions."

Well, crud. If I've ever wanted Willow Witch to magically appear somewhere, it was right there and then. Sam and I really had to put our heads together to remember which bottle was witch—I mean, which.

I pointed out the potion of leaping, which I used back in June to "fly" with my parrot. Oh, and as

soon as we unscrewed the caps on the bottles,
I knew the potion of invisibility. That one stinks
to the Nether and back because it's brewed with
fermented spider eyes. BLECH.

"This one is potion of fire resistance," said Sam. "I
remember because it's orange like fire." He seemed
pretty proud of himself.

Harold stared at that bottle as if it were the only
bottle of water left in the whole desert. I guess he
was wishing he'd had potion of fire resistance about

half an hour ago, when some of his husks caught on fire.

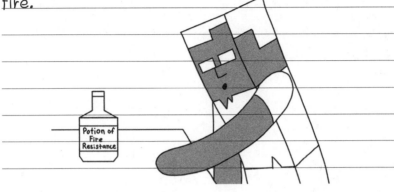

But Mr. Ender? He stared at that bottle with a different look in his eyes. He quickly screwed the cap back on and tucked the bottle in his pocket.

"Boys," he said, "tomorrow we're competing in Fire Building. And those Illagers are going up in SMOKE."

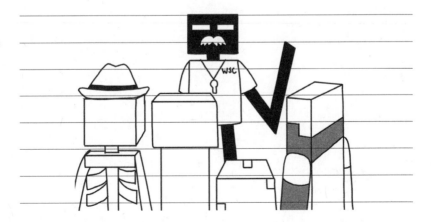

Well, alright, Mr. Ender. After getting jumped by Johnny Vindicator in the woods—and having the gunpowder scared out of me by those nasty Evokers and their Vexes—all I can say is . . .

GAME ON.

DAY 8: SUNDAY

I didn't know what Mr. Ender had in store for those Illagers until we woke up for dinner last night. Honest, I didn't!

See, I was looking forward to hitting up the Dining Hall for some chops and potatoes. I gotta say, the food here is WAY better than the crummy camp food you read about in books. Me and my stomach were practically sprinting to be first in line.

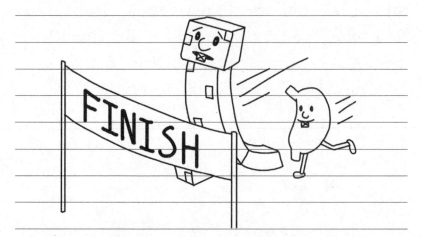

But Mr. Ender stopped me the way he always does: by teleporting straight into my path. "Harold," he said, "I'm going to need your help."

Turns out, he needed my FIREWORKS too. (I was wondering when my long-lost rockets were going to turn up.) Mr. Ender pulled them out of a bag and said that my cabin buddies and I were supposed to creep over to the Illager cabins and load up their fire pits with rockets. "Cover them up good with twigs and leaves," he said.

Well, I wasn't crazy about that plan. I'd finally been reunited with my rockets, and now I was supposed to practically GIVE them to the Illagers? But then I caught the gleam in Mr. Ender's eyes, and I played out his plan in my mind. I saw those Illagers building their fires during tonight's contest, and then I saw those firework rockets EXPLODING into the sky, and THEN I saw the fear on the Illagers' faces.

And I said, "Mr. Ender, sign me right up."

Sam didn't want to do it. I could tell by the way he
got all wiggly. "Gerald," he whispered, "remember
what happened at Mob Mall?"

Well, now, why did he have to bring THAT up? I
mean, sure, I did practically burn down the Mob Mall
back in June because of a "firework incident." But I
learned a lot from that experience—like, don't set
off rockets from a stand made of wood.

I think Sam has just gone soft on those Evokers and
doesn't want to make them mad. But that minecart
has already left the station, you know? So I told
Sam that this was just payback for what they and

their Vindicator buddies did to us. Besides, how do you say no to an Enderman?

I never did get to eat those chops down at the Dining Hall. But I DID get to take a big, gross-tasting gulp of potion of fire resistance. Mr. Ender made us all take a swig.

Then when it was time to see which cabin could start a fire the quickest, he set me to work with the flint and steel. I gotta say, rubbing a little steel handle against a piece of flint is a DUMB way to make a fire. Didn't anyone have a bucket of lava around here?

Nope. I rubbed that flint and steel as HARD as I could, but I could barely make a spark. Sam took over and made things worse, because he started sweating slime all over our kindling. And everyone KNOWS it's impossible to start a fire with wet wood.

Harold was too freaked out to take a turn after—you know—catching on fire last night. So it was up to Duke to take this thing home.

I'm not even sure he was using the steel. He might have been rubbing his own bony finger against the flint. But, whatever . . . the thing sparked, and when he held a piece of wool toward the spark, it started to smoke.

I would have been *have* been REALLY excited about that,
except I could see smoke rising from the Evokers'
fire pit, too. And then from the Vindicators' fire
pit. And that meant that ANY moment now . . . Yep,
you guessed it.

FIREWORKS!!!

We didn't even get our fire going before rockets
were screeching right and left across that night sky.
Except we forgot one thing: the Dark Forest is so

thick, you can't even SEE the sky. Which means the rockets weren't flying through the air. They were flying into TREES. I'm pretty sure one of them flew through a cabin window, too, because I heard glass break.

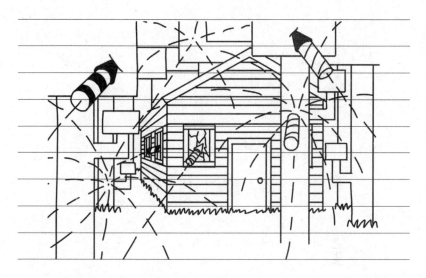

A bunch of the Illagers started cheering, which was NOT the reaction I expected. But they all shut right up when we heard an explosion in one of the cabins. And then? Something else . . . the crackle of a fire. A really BIG fire. A FOREST FIRE.

I guess Mr. Ender had forgotten that those trees were filled with dead leaves and dry branches. And that's how our fire-building contest turned into a fire-EXTINGUISHING contest.

It took all night to put out those fires! And a LOT of water, which we had to lug in buckets from the Dining Hall. We managed to save the Evokers' cabin, but they'll be sleeping in some REALLY wet bunk beds for a while.

As for the Vindicators? Well, let's just say it's a good thing they know how to build shelters.

The whole camp is a wet, smoky, stinky mess. We didn't win the fire-building contest, because our cabin didn't even get our fire GOING. But we do have the only dry cabin left standing at camp, so . . . that makes us winners, right?

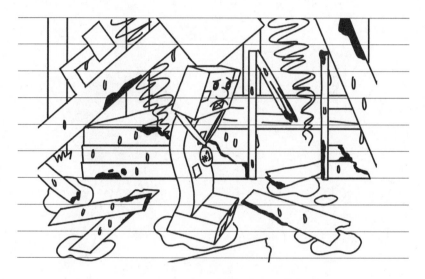

Except I wasn't really feeling like a winner this morning when a Vindicator threatened my life. Yep, you heard me right. It went down like this:

I was in the bathroom, trying to wipe the ashes off my face. This Vindicator walked by and whispered something in my ear. He uncrossed his arms JUST

enough for me to get a glimpse of his shiny axe,
and then he said:

"Creep, you and your firework-crafting SLIME friend
are going DOWN."

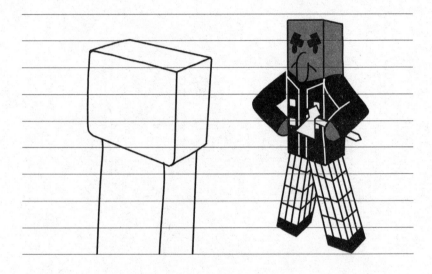

I almost ran after him to correct him. I mean, SAM
didn't make those fireworks. And he didn't even
want to use them! So, you know, threaten me all you
want, but leave Sam out of it.

I would have said all that, except my feet were glued to the bathroom floor. Something about those shiny axes TOTALLY freaks me out.

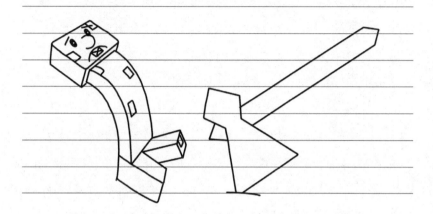

So instead, I high-tailed it back to the cabin to tell Sam that he had to watch his back—because after our little fire-building contest, there's a big red TARGET on it.

DAY 10: TUESDAY

I was almost GLAD to head out into the woods
Sunday night for the map-reading contest. At least
we could finally get away from those Vindicators,
who were holding a grudge just because we'd
burned down their cabin. SHEESH.

Everything started out okay. Mr. Ender gave us a
map and a compass. But when I looked at the map,
I thought it was all a big joke. I could see the red
X, which was supposed to be some sort of fake
"treasure." And I could see the little white dots
that were supposed to be US on the other side of
the map. But there was nothing in between!

"So, like, where is the trail we're supposed to take?" I finally worked up the nerve to ask.

"Start walking, Harold," said Mr. Ender, as if it were obvious. "If you're going in the right direction, the map will fill in."

I wanted to know why he couldn't just get us a filled-in map in the first place, but Mr. Ender isn't really big on lots of questions. Besides, he was already going on about how to figure out which direction you're moving in. "The sun rises in the east and sets in the west," he said. "And the clouds move from east to west. And the blah, biddy, blah, blah, blah . . ."

I tuned that part out because, you know, we HAD a compass that told us which way to go.

Sam held that and I held the map. Duke hummed a little tune to entertain us, and Harold . . . well, who knows where Harold was. He'd probably climbed the nearest mushroom and decided to stay put till we got back.

Just as we started covering some serious ground, Mr. Ender stopped us and said we should probably mark our trail so we could find our way back.

HUH? We had a map for crying out loud! But I kept my creeper mouth shut this time as Mr. Ender pulled these tufts of blue wool out of his pocket—the same ones we'd tried to light on fire yesterday. He said we should stick them on bushes and trees along the trail. "Just in case we lose the map," he said.

Boy, talk about a downer. Did he think I didn't know how to hang on to a lousy sheet of paper? Yep, that's what he thought alright. And knowing what I know now, I probably should have handed that map over to Duke—the dude with ten fingers who could really get a grip.

Anyway, I held the map, and Duke took the wool and started marking the trail. I kept my eyes on the map, and sure enough, as we walked toward that red X, our white dots got bigger, and the map started filling in. I could see the woods ahead, and a few giant mushrooms, and then . . . water! We were getting close to a lake or something. So it turns out Harold made a good call skipping out on this hike.

We wound around the lake, and that red X was getting closer and closer. And I started getting excited about the treasure. Why? I dunno. I mean, it wasn't the REAL treasure. We'd be finding that on Survival Night. So this was more like the prize you'd win at a carnival or something—like that stuffed Mooshroom that I just HAD to have, until I finally won it (after spending a gazillion emeralds). Now I don't even know where that Mooshroom is. I probably gave it to Cammy, who used it as a chew toy and ended up blowing off a couple of its legs during a temper tantrum.

Sure enough, when we finally saw the red flag marking the treasure, I could see that it was going to be a ginormous disappointment. Sam bounced toward the flag, and Duke rattled-walked right over. But by the time I got there, they both had these plastic water bottles that said "I survived Camp Woodland!" on them. WOO-HOO.

Sam wanted to fill his right away. (It sure doesn't take much to get that slime excited.) We walked back toward the lake, and he tossed me my water bottle. I lunged for it, and . . . well, that's when everything took a turn for the worse. Did I mention it was kind of a breezy night?

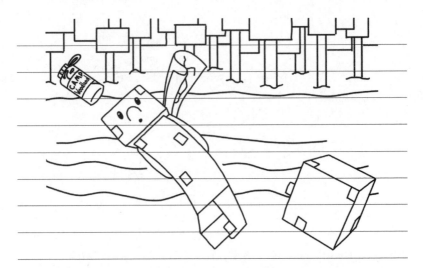

Yep, the wind caught the map I was carrying. And blew it toward the lake. And the water practically reached up and grabbed the map. (Maybe it was Harold's Drowneds or something, just messing with me.)

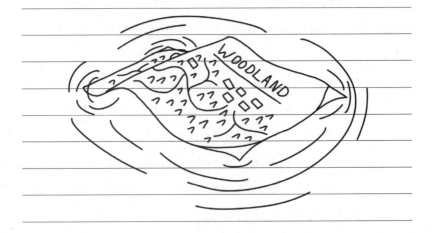

Sam was like, "No worries, Gerald! We marked the trail home, remember?"

So we started looking for those blue tufts of wool. But guess what? THERE WEREN'T ANY. We saw a RED tuft, but Mr. Ender said someone else left that— and it could lead ANYWHERE.

So we circled that lake three times looking for blue wool. By then, the sun was starting to come up, and Duke started getting jangly. Mr. Ender said that the trees grew so thick out there, that Duke PROBABLY wouldn't get burned. But Duke didn't seem very reassured—and I can't say that I really blame the guy.

So Mr. Ender said we had no choice but to "make camp." Except we hadn't really packed a tent, or sleeping bags, or pajamas. (What can I say? I'm a creeper who likes sleeping in his jammies.)

"You boys know how to build a shelter," Mr. Ender said. But let's face it—we really DIDN'T. And after fifteen minutes of hacking at branches with our pathetic pickaxes, we'd only managed to build one wall. It was enough to protect Duke from the sun, I guess. So we all picked a patch of grass and settled in for the day.

But I gotta say, I didn't sleep a WINK. Not ONE wink. Mom always says, "The sun will go down again tomorrow." But here's the thing: when that sun set, we'd STILL be lost out here by the lake. With no blue wool. No map. And no marked trail to lead us back to camp. So WHAT WERE WE GOING TO DO?

Yep, that was pretty much the low point of the map-reading contest. No, wait—there was a lower one.

When we finally got up, Mr. Ender had a genius idea. He said we should climb a hill to see if we could spot our cabins from up high. Well, I led the pack running up that hill. And sure enough, when we got to the top, I could see the rooftops of a couple of cabins way off in the distance. The real clue was the smoke still rising from the roof of the third one. That's how I knew I was looking at Woodland Survival Camp and not, like, Camp Golem or something. (Unless Chloe had managed to burn down a cabin, too.)

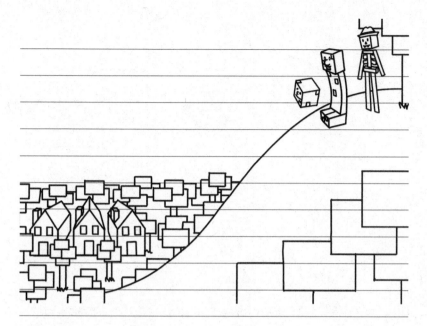

Anyway, we used our compass to hike back in the direction of those cabins. It took FOREVER, and we were super hungry. I was hoping we'd pass a huge mushroom along the way, but of course, when you're looking for one, they're nowhere to be found.

We finally made it back to camp. And that was when I spotted a blue tuft of wool stuck in a tree. So we hadn't totally lost our minds. We HAD marked the trail!

But just as I was reaching for the wool, I heard the strangest sound.

"WO-LO-LO!"

And right before my eyes, that blue wool changed to RED. I thought I was dreaming—until I heard cackling behind me. I spun around and found an Evoker, his arms raised above his head as if he had JUST cast a spell. A spell that changes blue wool to red?

Well, THAT explains why we couldn't follow our blue wool back to camp.

The more I think about it, the madder I get. I mean, we could have been lost in those woods for AGES! So forget Johnny the Vindicator. The Evokers just bumped up to number one on my Enemies List.

I can't believe that a week ago, I was freaked out about hanging out in the Dark Forest, where we could get gobbled up by a pack of hungry WOLVES.

But now, I'm starting to think there are scarier things than wolves. Like Evokers who attack us with spells every time we turn around.

Sure, we made it back to camp this time. But . . . what about NEXT time? Will my camp buddies and I even SURVIVE Survival Night?

All I can say is, it's time for Gerald Creeper Jr. to start coming up with some genius ideas. PRONTO.

DAY 11: WEDNESDAY

So I just found out that Survival Night is actually Survival NIGHTS. We have to spend TWO nights in the woods! Which I think is really unfair since my cabin buddies and I already spent an extra night out there. We should be getting BUKU bonus points for that.

Anyway, we leave tonight. Which means before dawn this morning, we gotta roll up our sleeping bags and pack up our tents. And prepare to meet our fate.

When mail got delivered, I was willing to give Mom
one more chance to prove her love. I crossed
my toes, hoping that she'd finally sent me a care
package—you know, since this might be her last
chance to communicate with me. EVER.

Sam's mom sent him a whole pack of smoked salmon
to take into the woods. I'm a little worried about
him smelling like a giant green fish. I mean, talk
about WOLF BAIT. But at least he'll go out knowing
his family loved him.

Me? All I _have_ to take into the woods is a postcard of Cammy riding on a dolphin's back. Does she even KNOW that her big brother may be about to perish?

Nope. She probably doesn't even remember my name.

The one thing that gives me hope is that Mr. Ender is packing our potions. The potion of invisibility will sure come in handy if a pack of wolves shows up. And the potion of leaping could help us leap over those huge mushrooms—or any giant fangs that sprout—in a single bound.

Oh, plus, Mr. Ender gave Sam back his slime balls. See, after we found out Evokers could change the color of wool, those trail markers didn't seem so useful anymore. So Mr. Ender says Sam should

smear a little slime on birch trees along the trail.
NO mob can get slime off bark—that stuff sticks
like glue.

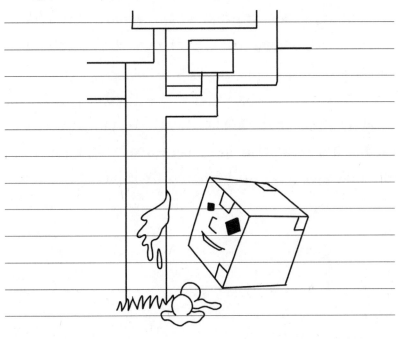

So we've got a couple of things going for us. But
I gotta say, there's this pit of dread in my gut
that's spinning like a mob in a spawner. Something
BAD's going to happen—I can feel it. But WHAT?

And if I don't know what it is, how can I come up with a genius way to save the day?

Meanwhile, Sam is stinking up the cabin with smoked salmon and grinning like a geek over tonight's big "adventure."

But you know what REALLY stinks? Being the only mob in the room that has a clue what's going down. And not having a clue how to STOP it.

SIGH.

DAY 12: THURSDAY MORNING

OUCH.

I'm trying to sleep, but I've got cactus prickers poking me in the rear. NO, they don't grow in the Dark Forest. But I guess Mom and Dad didn't wash my sleeping bag after our trip to the desert last summer. I'm pretty sure I've got sand stuck to my feet, too. That'll feel GREAT when I have to put on my boots and start hiking again.

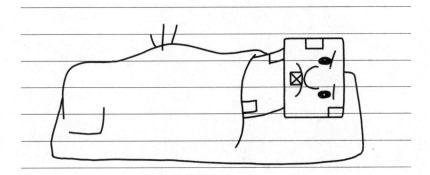

Which probably won't be anytime soon, because we only hiked for about an hour before we hit a

stream, and Harold would NOT take another step.
But let me back up and tell you how we got here.

We got our new map—the one with the REAL
treasure marked on it. Except instead of a red X,
there was this little house. So I guess the treasure
is hidden in a house. Mr. Ender even told us what the
treasure was so we'd be on the lookout for it. It's
some sort of gold statue called a Totem of Undying.

And the first cabin to snag it and get it back to camp wins EVERYTHING (or at least a pizza party).

So we were heading toward that little house on the map, with Duke using the compass and Sam marking slime on every birch tree he could find. I had a tight grip on that map, let me tell you. But as the map started to fill in, I could see water coming up ahead. And from over my shoulder, HAROLD saw it, too.

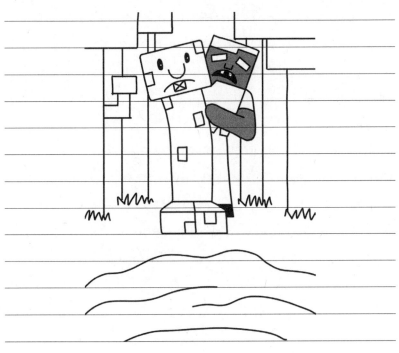

The husk practically jumped on my back, he was so scared. And when we got to the edge of the water, he REFUSED to cross it. I'm sure he could picture those Drowned mobs at the bottom of the stream, swimming up to grab our feet and pull us down with them.

I was hoping Mr. Ender would just let the poor husk go back to camp. But he said we had to stick together—that on Survival Night, no mob gets left behind. So we WAITED. And TRIED to get Harold to cross. Mr. Ender even tried to teleport him across, but I guess husks don't really get around that way.

By the time Harold got some courage up, dawn was breaking, and then we had a whole OTHER problem on our hands. Duke started sweating, like he was going to catch fire any second. So we finally had to pitch our tent and call it a night.

I'm trying to rap myself to sleep, but meanwhile,
I'm SURE the other cabins have already reached
that little house on the map. The Illagers are
probably throwing a party there, dancing around
with their Totem of Undying, and laughing at us
poor, pathetic mobs who aren't even halfway
there.

Husk hates water
He won't go
Duke hates sunlight
Burns up, yo.

Can't move forward,
Stuck right here.
Sandy feet and
Prickers in my rear.
OUCH.

Oh, well. At least we haven't been hit by an Evoker curse yet. But, hey, the day is still young . . .

DAY 12: THURSDAY NIGHT

Mom says that things always look better at night, when the sun goes down. Like, if you go to bed worried, you usually wake up feeling better.

Except that was NOT how things went down tonight. I woke up thinking that FINALLY we could cross that stream. That Harold would be feeling brave. And we could get a move on and try to make up for lost time.

But Harold was NOT feeling brave. And it turned out, MR. ENDER wasn't either. I gotta say, there's nothing that freaks me out MORE than when the grown-up in charge starts freaking out. And that's what happened when the rain came.

Did you know Endermen REALLY don't like rain?

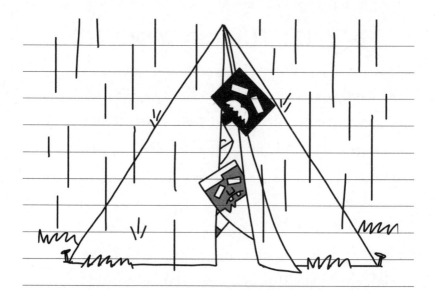

I sort of knew it—my buddy Eddy Enderman back home pretty much sits out rainy school nights. But I NEVER in a gazillion years expected our counselor, scary Mr. Ender, to be spooked by a few raindrops.

You should have seen the guy. He practically dug a hole in the ground when the rain started pitter-pattering down on our tent. And then he said something that my ears can never UN-hear. He said, "You boys are going to have to go on without us."

Say WHAT? What happened to "leave no mob behind"?

Mr. Ender yammered on about how Sam, Duke, and I had plenty of "survival skills." That we just had to remember everything he'd taught us (which, honestly, I couldn't remember a LICK of at that moment). He finished with, "Our cabin is depending on you. Make us proud."

Well, CRUD. I didn't buy into any of that hooey, but Sam puffed up like a pufferfish and was all like, "Yes, sir, we've got this." And Duke stood up beside him. And that's how we found ourselves hiking down a trail WITHOUT a grown-up.

I mean, Duke had the compass. And I had the map. But I felt like we were heading off to fight the Ender Dragon without any weapons. Then I remembered that we DID have weapons, sort of. We had potions—strapped to Sam's back. So as soon as we crossed the stream, we pulled out those bottles and figured out a plan.

The way I saw it, we had to cover as much ground
as we could before dawn broke and the sun came
up again. So we all took a swig of potion of leaping.
It wasn't exactly like flying, but pretty soon, the
three of us were leaping through the woods,
bouncing off giant mushrooms and soaring through
the trees. It was the MOST fun I've had at camp so
far, I gotta say. And I could tell Sam and Duke were
having a blast too.

But the potion eventually wore off. SIGH. And then we were all pretty worn out. So we're taking a break now, resting on a giant mushroom and figuring out our next move.

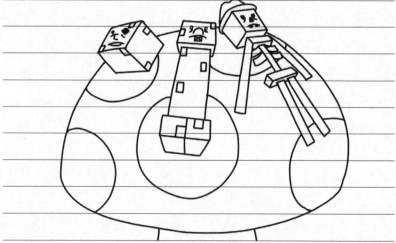

The map says that if we keep going southeast, we'll hit that little house by dawn. So as soon as my buddies are ready, we're going to get a move on. If I squint, I can ALMOST see that gold statue in the distance. This contest isn't over YET.

DAY 12: THURSDAY NIGHT (CONTINUED)

Aw, crud. CRUD, CRUD, CRUD!!!

We lost our compass.

I know. It freaks me out just to write the words. But
don't panic. That's what I keep telling myself. Sam
is sitting on a mushroom snacking on smoked salmon,
as if all's right with the Overworld. And I'm trying to
keep it that way, because the LAST thing I need is
that slime going all anxious and jittery on me.

But Duke looks as worried as I feel. Or maybe he just looks guilty. Because while he was leaping, he SOMEHOW let go of that compass. He doesn't even know WHERE exactly. But it's long gone now, so no use crying over spilled lava.

For just a second, there was a glimmer of hope. Duke reminded me that Mr. Ender taught us OTHER ways of figuring out which direction we were going. "With the sun," Duke said. "The sun sets in the west, so if we can just find the setting sun . . ."

We both looked up. But those trees were so dense, we couldn't even see the MOON.

Then I remembered the other thing Mr. Ender had said. "The clouds move east to west," I said.

We looked up again. But we could see the clouds about as easily as we could see the moon. There was nothing but TREES overhead. So, thanks, Mr. Ender. Thanks a LOT for the super-helpful tips.

It was Sam who bounced off the mushroom and said we should just climb a hill. "Like last time," he said, reminding us how we'd climbed a hill during the map-reading contest to find our way back to camp.

Well, DUH. Every once in a while, the slime surprises me. He led the way up the nearest hill, which turned into a really STEEP hill, with a SUPER-slippery trail because of all the rain. I might have pulled ahead of Sam once or twice, because if I fall backward, I'd MUCH rather land on a soft slime than a bony skeleton. But by the time we reached the top, we could see the moon overhead.

And when we looked down the other side of the hill, we could see something ELSE.

Yep, I'm pretty sure THAT is the house we've been looking for. It's tiny on our map, but now that we're closer, I can tell there's nothing tiny about it.

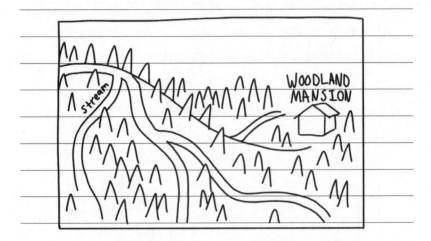

And if we get a move on RIGHT NOW, we can make it there before dawn!

DAY 13: FRIDAY MORNING

So I'm not a superstitious creeper. Like, even though this is our 13th day at camp, I'm pretty sure we're having GOOD luck right now—not bad. I mean, even if a black cat crossed our path, I wouldn't bat an eye (even though I REALLY don't like cats). Because we made it to the house before the sun came up. And guess what else? We found BEDS to sleep in!

The house is really more like a MANSION. It's three stories tall, and filled with a winding maze of hallways and a gazillion rooms. We're just going to rest for an hour or two, and then we're going to find _that_ Totem of Undying.

Sam and Duke are already cashed out on a big bed in the middle of the room. Well, it LOOKED big until Sam crawled in. Poor Duke is probably going to fall off any second now. I'm a "sleep solo" kind of guy, so I climbed the ladder to the loft and found another bed just my size. PERFECT.

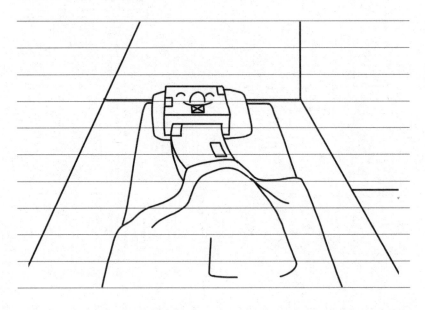

I know I should be catching a few winks after the night we had. But who can sleep at a time like this? Well, SAM can. The slime is snoring.

Whoa, WAIT. I just heard something else. Is that the door creaking open . . . ?

DAY 13: FRIDAY MORNING (CONTINUED)

THEY TOOK SAM AND DUKE!!!

This house is SWARMING with Illagers! I should have KNOWN an empty house was too good to be true!

They must have waited till we were in bed. Poor Sam didn't stand a chance. While those Vindicators were dragging him out of the room, he was practically still sleeping.

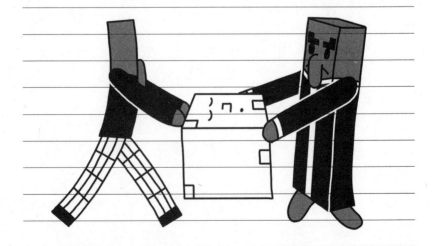

Duke woke up, but the skeleton didn't put up a fight—like I said, he's just a bag of bones.

I know—I SHOULD have done something. I should have leaped off the loft and tackled one of those Vindicators. I should have hollered or thrown a potion or SOMETHING.

But I didn't. I froze. And I'm not proud, let me tell you.

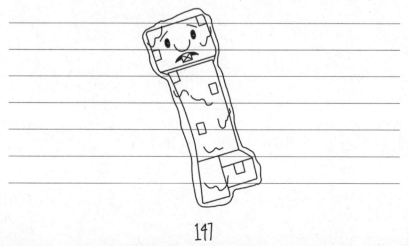

As soon as the Vindicators were gone, I snuck out of bed and tried to follow them.

I crept down the hall, listening for voices. But this place is so HUGE. And who knows how many MORE Vindicators are here?

I feel like a silverfish that crawled straight into a spider's web. I'm stuck—I can't leave without Sam and Duke. But how am I supposed to go up against a whole group of Vindicators? WITHOUT Mr. Ender?

"Use your brains."

That wasn't Mom's voice. It was my own—reminding me that I may not have survival skills, but I DO have some smarts. And I AM a creeper, after all.

So I crept back into the bedroom and snagged the potion of invisibility out of Sam's backpack. I grabbed a few slime balls, too. Then I crept back down the hall DETERMINED to check every room in this mansion until I found my buddies—and rescued them.

I found rooms filled with flowerpots. I found more bedrooms, and a library. I found a storage room FILLED with chests. Then I found a room that scared the gunpowder right out of me.

Remember when I said I was feeling lucky—and wouldn't even care if a black cat crossed my path? Well, let's just say one DID. A GIANT black cat, ready to pounce. I thought it was real when I opened the door to that room, and I nearly blew right out of my creeper skin. Then I saw it was a statue. And it looked kind of like Sam's cat, Moo. That made me MISS Sam. So I shut the door and kept going. Like I said, I'll search this place top to bottom till I find my buddies.

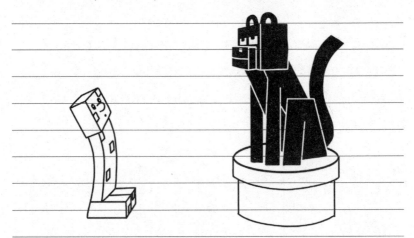

That's about the time I heard VOICES. I really had to creep when I reached the big dining hall and saw ILLAGERS sitting around a table. Guess who'd joined the Vindicators there? A bunch of EVOKERS. So those mobs were working together now—AGAINST

my buddies and me. Did I mention that life is
TOTALLY unfair?

I didn't see ONE counselor in that dining hall.
So somehow, these Illagers had given their own
counselors the slip. I don't know if I felt relieved
about that, or horrified.

Then I saw something else on the long dining table.
Something gold. Something shiny. The Totem of
Undying! The Illagers had found it! I was so close to
that statue now, I could imagine what it felt like. I
could imagine GRABBING it. But the Illagers weren't
going to give it up without a fight.

Besides, first things first. I had to find my buddies. THEN we could worry about getting the statue.

So I spied on the Illagers as long as it took—and finally they said five words that were MUSIC to my ears: "We put them in JAIL."

They HAD to be talking about Sam and Duke. So somewhere in this mansion was a jail cell where I could find my buddies. I decided to work my way DOWN. I mean, where else would a jail be except for in the basement?

I didn't need a compass to head south. I just had to find a cobblestone staircase. And when I did, I took those steps two by two. I'm pretty sure I blew through a few spider webs, but I didn't care. Time was a'ticking.

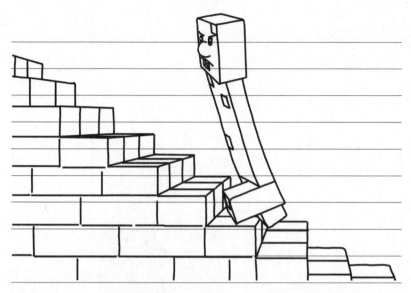

Before I knew it, I was there—crouched in front
of a jail cell door. And from inside, I could HEAR
Sam whimpering. He was probably crying huge, slimy
tears. And was that the sound of Duke rattling? Or a
set of jail keys?

I couldn't figure out how to get in—until I saw
Redstone dust leading to a lever. I was about to
pull it, too. But then I saw I wasn't alone down here

in the hall. Nope. There was a Vindicator guarding
that jail cell.

JOHNNY.

DAY 13: FRIDAY NIGHT

Sometimes back home when I'm playing Humancraft, I just hit the RESTART button. I mean, sometimes, you've messed up a game so bad, you don't know how to fix it.

That's how I feel right now.

See, I did NOT rescue my buddies from the jail cell this morning. Instead, I got thrown INTO it. While I was spying on Johnny, ANOTHER Vindicator was creeping toward me. And the whole day since, I've been sitting beside Sam, wondering where I went wrong in life.

"We're never gonna get out." That's what Duke keeps saying. "We're gonna rot in here, till we're nothing but skin and bones!"

Was he JOKING with me? Nope. The dude was dead serious.

"Duke, you could probably fit through those bars," I tried telling him. "What are you waiting for? Save yourself!"

But his head just drooped, looking way too big for his bony body. And Sam is still blubbering up a storm. If this keeps up, I'm going to lose my cool, too. SOMEONE has to keep it together.

Think, creep. Think!

Duke and I might be able to squeeze through those bars. But Sam will NEVER fit. And we're NOT leaving him behind.

So . . . hmm.

Okay, I've got it. It's not the best plan in the world, but right now, it's the only one we've got. See, maybe we don't HAVE to squeeze out through those bars. Maybe we just have to make it LOOK like we did.

Time to pack you up, my trusty journal. And bring on the potion of invisibility.

DAY 13: FRIDAY NIGHT (CONTINUED)

WHOA.

My heart is still POUNDING in my chest. Or maybe that's SAM's heart. We're squished together in a giant mushroom right now, so it's hard to tell where his slime body ends and my creeper body begins.

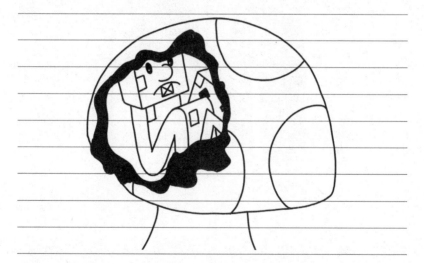

WOW, do I have a lot to catch you up on.

Remember the potion of invisibility? Well, that worked like a charm. It was hard to get Duke and

Sam to drink it. I mean, the mobs had pretty much
GIVEN UP on life. But I waited for the perfect
time. And finally, an Evoker came down to the jail
cell, and Johnny struck up a good long conversation
with him.

Right away, we each took a swig of that disgusting-
tasting potion. I didn't FEEL any different, but when
I looked down at my feet, I watched them s-l-o-w-
l-y disappear. I couldn't see Sam or Duke anymore
either!

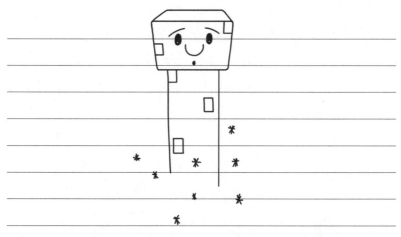

And when that Evoker glanced toward us, he
FREAKED right out. He got all mad at Johnny for
letting us slip away. They pulled that Redstone
lever, and the jail door swung open, and they
rushed in to see if we had tunneled our way out.
And that's when we made our move.

I RACED out of the jail, hoping Sam wouldn't bounce off one of the Illagers and give our plan away. I heard Duke rattling behind me, so I kept going. I led my buddies back up the cobblestone stairs, all the way down the hall to the dining room. And when I saw that the Totem of Undying was still there, I snatched the thing RIGHT out from under the Evokers' potato-shaped noses.

Except I wasn't QUITE fast enough. Because the potion was already wearing off! I could see the bottom half of Sam's body wiggling and jiggling across the room.

UH-OH.

The Evokers raised their hands—and I knew exactly
what that meant.

I was almost RELIEVED to see the Vexes appear
instead of those NASTY fangs. "Don't look at them!"
I told Sam. "Just ignore them!" I hollered at Duke.

And we did. We left those flying mobs behind and
whipped down the hall. I caught a glimpse of a

Vindicator chasing us with a ginormous axe, but after that, I didn't look back again. Some things you're just better off NOT knowing.

Somehow, we made it out of that house without getting caught. At least we THOUGHT we had.

But just a ways down the trail, an Evoker caught up with us. He must have been casting some new kind of spell, because his robes were blue now. And he was carrying a bow and arrow. YIKES.

I whipped the only weapon at him that I could find in my backpack: a SLIME ball. Sam caught on, and he started whipping them, too. But as soon as Sam hit the Evoker, the mob raised his arms and waved them in the air. A black plume of smoke rose from his hands, and suddenly . . . Sam was shrieking. Had he been hit?

I whipped more slime balls at the Evoker until he backed up, away from Sam. But then he waved his arms again and disappeared. When he came back, he had THREE buddies beside him.

We were outnumbered now. And Sam was still hollering something. Finally, I could make out his words: "I. Can't. See!"

HUH?

Sure enough, the slime was blind as a bat! Duke and I grabbed him, one of us on either side, and rushed him into the woods. It's not easy to squeeze through a dense forest beside a wide slime. But I could hear the Evokers behind us shooting arrows. Thwack, thwack, thwack! So we ran faster. I'm pretty sure we were CARRYING Sam by then. But when your buddy's in trouble, you do what you have to do.

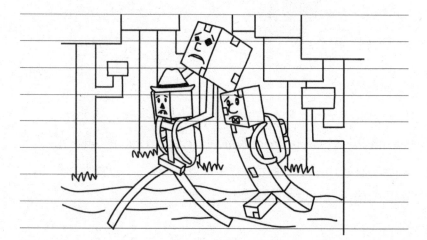

Then I saw the giant mushroom. It rose before us like a mirage—like a trick our eyes were playing on us. But it was real.

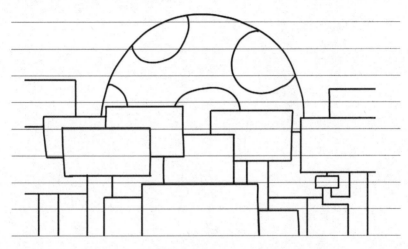

We ran around to the other side, and I could tell it had already started to rot. The insides were soft and mushy—easy to scoop out.

"Get inside!" I hollered to Sam after I'd carved out enough room. Then I squeezed in beside him. And Duke did, too.

Now I'm not gonna lie—it STINKS in here. But the Evokers have gone quiet. So maybe they don't know where we are. Maybe they've given up, taken their arrows, and gone back to the mansion.

I'm crossing my toes.

Sam just nudged me. "I can see again!" he said.

Well, HALLELUJAH. I was starting to wonder how Duke and I were going to get Sam back to the cabin if he couldn't even see the trees right in front of his face.

So maybe it's time to move on now. Except . . . which way do we go?

I'm pretty sure Sam stopped marking the trail with slime a long time ago. We have NO compass. And the map in my backpack only shows where we were going—not how to get back.

HUH.

Survival Night #2 is shaping up to be the LONGEST night of my life.

DAY 14: SATURDAY MORNING

It was Sam who said we should follow the wolf tracks.

Now you KNOW that idea would have never come out of my mouth. But Sam's an animal-loving kind of mob. And it turns out, Duke was WAY more afraid of the sun coming up than he was of a wolf. I guess skeletons are pretty good at taming wolves—because, you know, they can just throw them a bone.

Anyway, Sam and Duke pointed out that we had to cross the stream in order to get back to camp. But we couldn't cross the stream if we couldn't FIND it. And the wolf tracks might LEAD us there.

So I finally gave in. But I let Sam lead the way. And Duke brought up the rear. Yep, I'd stuck out my creeper neck ENOUGH in the last twenty-four hours. I was ready to be the sandwich fixin's instead of the bread.

We followed the tracks for AGES. (Or maybe it just felt that way because I was holding my breath.) But GUESS WHAT? Mr. Ender had taught us something useful after all, because those tracks DID lead to the stream! Just in time, too. Sunlight was starting to trickle down through the tree branches.

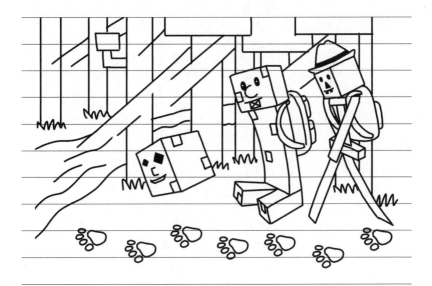

I was *hoping* that Mr. Ender and Harold would still be there, waiting for us. But they must have headed back to camp. So we found our lousy shelter—the wall made out of twigs—and now we're settling down to sleep.

I've got the Totem of Undying right here in my sleeping bag. If an Illager shows up to steal it, they're going to have to take ME, too. Because my buddies and I are so close to victory now, I can SMELL it.

DAY 14: SATURDAY NIGHT

Sometimes, a creep doesn't recognize Death when he's staring it in the face.

See, it turns out those Evokers we ran into when we left the mansion WEREN'T Evokers after all! But we didn't know that until we made it back to camp tonight, thank Golem.

A campfire was blazing—and a ring of Evokers and Vindicators sat around the fire. At first, I was annoyed. I mean, how could they all sit there as if NOTHING had happened? As if they hadn't thrown us in a jail cell back at that mansion, and chased us with a bunch of vexes, and shot arrows at us with bows, and cast spells that made Sam go BLIND for a while?

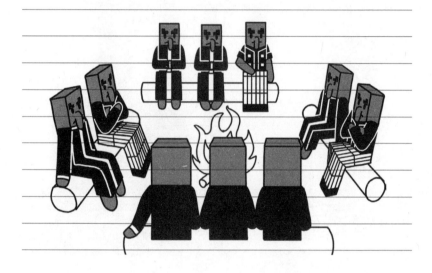

I must have been tired and crabby, because I hollered all of that at the Illagers—and more. I expected them to holler back, or cast some dumb spells to shut me up. But they didn't.

Johnny the Vindicator uncrossed his arms, dropped his axe, and said, "Wait, YOU guys actually fought an Illusioner?"

I had no idea what he was talking about. Then I remembered the ghost story he'd told around this campfire a week ago—which felt like a YEAR ago. Well, I didn't want to hear it. He wasn't going to fool me with that crud.

Except I noticed that the OTHER Illagers looked pretty impressed with us, too. Even the two Vindicator counselors who walked over from the cabin. "How'd you fight off the Illusioner?" one of them asked.

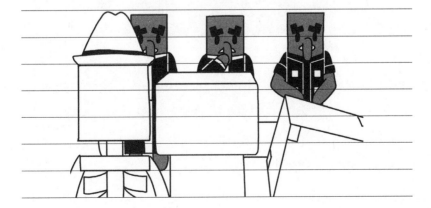

"With slime balls," Sam said proudly.

"And a giant mushroom," added Duke.

You should have heard the oohs and ahhs that rolled around that campfire. You'd have thought we killed the Ender Dragon or something.

Then I saw two purple eyes peering at me through the darkness—and I have NEVER been happier to see Mr. Ender teleport to my side, let me tell you. I practically hugged the dude.

Right away, I pulled the golden statue out of my backpack. "Totem of Undying," I announced proudly.

Mr. Ender's eyes glowed so bright, I almost had to look away. "You did well, Harold," he said.

"Harold"? REALLY???

That's when Harold Husk showed up—keeping a safe distance from the fire this time.

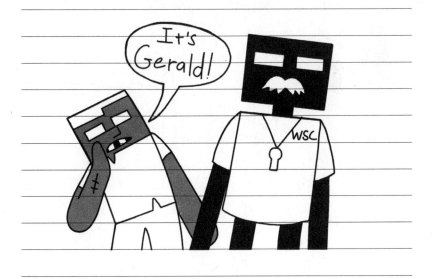

I appreciated that. I mean, now that I wasn't getting in trouble anymore, it was kind of nice to get a little credit for a change.

Mr. Ender patted me on the back, and Sam and Duke, too. Then he told ALL the other Illagers that me and my buddies were TRUE survivors.

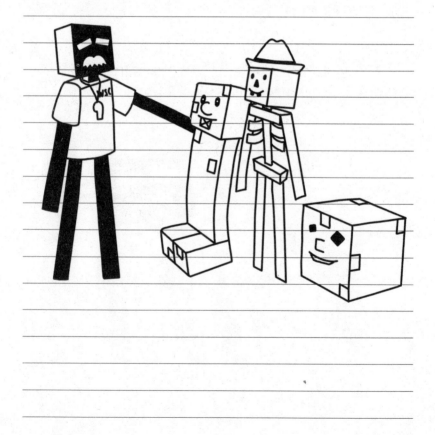

Well, I don't know about that. I never did learn how to build a decent shelter, but I can tunnel my way into a giant mushroom when I have to. I'm still afraid of wolves, but I'll track one just far enough to find water. And I can read a map, even if I can't see the sun or tell which way the wind is blowing.

But if Mr. Ender REALLY wants to hear which survival tip saved my creeper butt, I'll tell him it was this one: "Leave no mob behind."

Because I'm pretty sure that without Sam and Duke, I'd still be stuck in the woods somewhere. Or hiding out in that giant rotten mushroom.

Anyway, I'm crashing early tonight, way before dawn. Because Mom and Dad are picking me up tomorrow—at least I HOPE they remember to come get me. I've sure got some stories for them.

DAY 15: SUNDAY

Mom and Dad were a sight for sore eyes when they showed up at Woodland Survival Camp tonight. Dad had a SERIOUS moonburn—I guess the guy fell asleep on the beach a few times too many.

Chloe was with them, too, wearing her Golem Scout sash. It was full of badges, and I'm sure she wanted me to gush over them and ask how she'd earned them. But I didn't. I mean, Sam, Duke, and I had a golden statue with our names engraved on it sitting in the Woodland Survival Camp trophy case. So I didn't feel jealous at all, thank you very much.

I wasn't even all that jealous of my parents' beach vacation anymore—especially after Mom said Cammy, the Exploding Baby, had blown up on a boat and gotten them all kicked off the island. HUH. Imagine that.

Dad must have felt guilty or something, because he said that if I WANTED to, we could all take a family camping trip together next week, before school started.

CAMPING?

No way. I've had my fill of camping lately. Besides, my buddy Sam is heading home, so I'm going home, too. We mobs gotta stick together, you know.

It's kind of a survival thing.

DON'T MISS ANY OF GERALD CREEPER JR.'S HILARIOUS ADVENTURES!

Sky Pony Press
New York

DON'T MISS ANY OF GERALD CREEPER JR.'S HILARIOUS ADVENTURES!

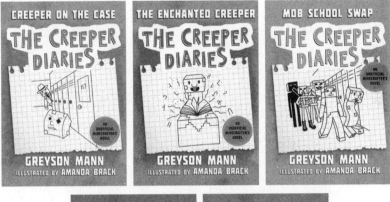

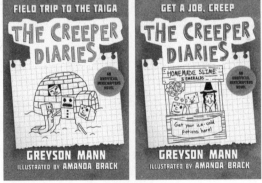

Sky Pony Press
New York